THE REAL GHOSTBUSTERS
The Great Ghost Show

Written by Michael Teitelbaum
Illustrated by Steve Smallwood

LITTLE SIMON

Simon & Schuster Building, Rockefeller Center
1230 Avenue of the Americas, New York, New York 10020

Editorial services by Parachute Press, Inc.
Copyright © 1987 by Columbia Pictures Television, a division of CPT Holdings, Inc.
THE REAL GHOSTBUSTERS™ Copyright © 1986 by Columbia Pictures Television, a division of CPT Holdings, Inc.
GHOSTBUSTERS™ Copyright © 1984 by Columbia Pictures Industries, Inc.
Manufactured in the United States of America

10 9 8 7 6 5 4 3 2

ISBN: 0-671-64569-2

"**N**o, Peter, not like that," said Egon Spengler. "Use these three fingers." Egon and his fellow Real Ghostbusters, Peter Venkman, Ray Stantz, and Winston Zeddmore, were in the old firehouse that served as their headquarters. The group was watching TV and eating take-out Chinese food. Egon was instructing his friends in the fine art of eating with chopsticks.

"I give up!" shouted Peter, throwing the chopsticks over his head and grabbing the nearest fork. "It's impossible to eat with these things."

Slimer, The Real Ghostbusters' pet ghost, caught the sticks and gobbled them up.

"*Slimer* knows how to handle chopsticks," laughed Winston. "No problem."

The Real Ghostbusters turned their attention back to the TV set. The weatherman on the screen pointed at his map, and suddenly it began to snow—right in the studio!

"Hey! What's going on?" wondered Winston, as he flipped the channel. On one channel a newscaster was floating above her desk, and the music videos on another channel were running backwards, at double speed.

"This is really weird," said Peter.

"It seems to be affecting all the TV stations in the city," added Egon.

Sure enough, something strange was happening on every channel they turned to. On a cooking show, a pie flew up and hit the cook right in the face. When The Real Ghostbusters flipped to a game show, all the buzzers lit at the same time, and the car that they were giving away drove off by itself.

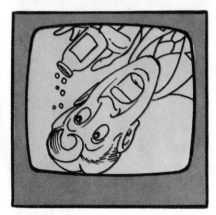

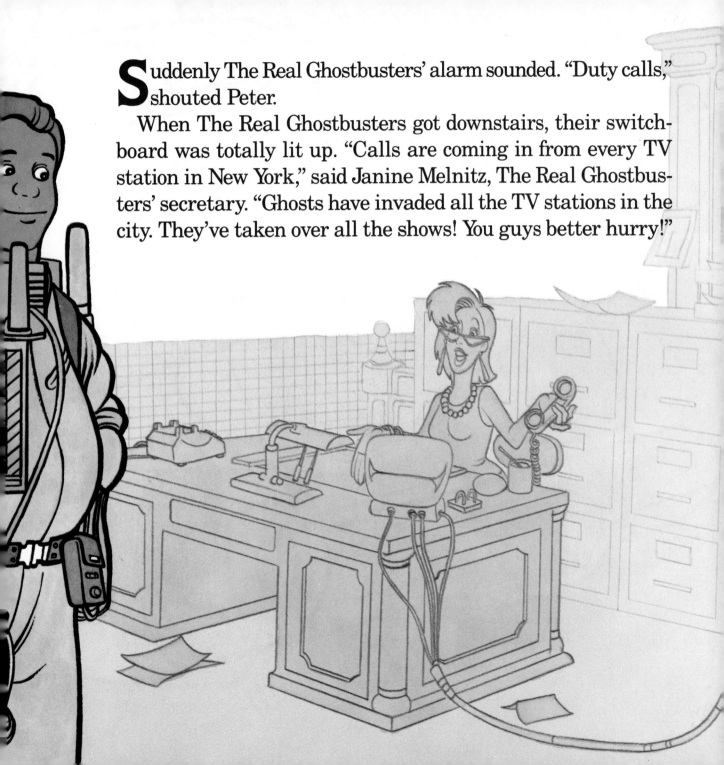

S uddenly The Real Ghostbusters' alarm sounded. "Duty calls," shouted Peter.

When The Real Ghostbusters got downstairs, their switchboard was totally lit up. "Calls are coming in from every TV station in New York," said Janine Melnitz, The Real Ghostbusters' secretary. "Ghosts have invaded all the TV stations in the city. They've taken over all the shows! You guys better hurry!"

The Real Ghostbusters grabbed their Proton Packs and raced to Ecto 1, their supercharged ghost-chasing vehicle. Off they sped through the streets of New York City.

"Where are we going first?" asked Ray.

"To the studios of WZBS, the city's largest TV station," replied Egon. "We'll start there."

ON AIR !

Even the Real Ghostbusters were not prepared for the sight that greeted them when they arrived at the studios of WZBS. There were ghosts everywhere! All types of ghosts! Some looked like clowns, some like soap opera stars, and others like game show hosts. There were rock singer ghosts and TV Mom ghosts! They were up in the lights, behind the cameras, and in the dressing rooms. Everywhere!

"**R**eady, guys?" began Peter. "Let's bring the curtain down on this ghostly show."

"Arm Proton Guns, Ghostbusters," ordered Egon. "Let's go!"

The Real Ghostbusters whipped into action, chasing ghosts

around the studio, firing Particle Streams. Though they tried
their best, in a few minutes they realized that it was hopeless.
Every time they thought the job was done, more ghosts appeared
in another room.

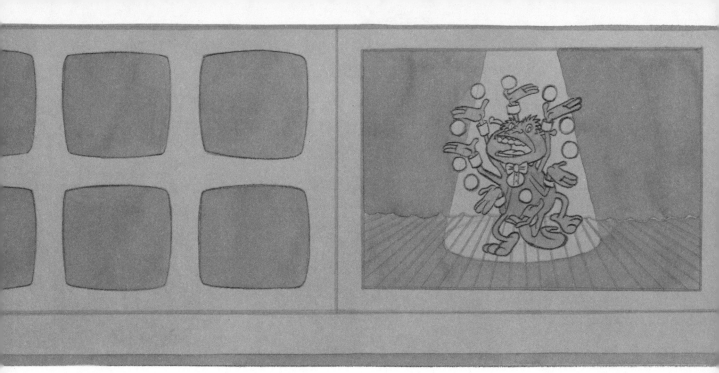

Just then, a nervous little man with a beard came over and introduced himself. "I'm John Schmidt, the station manager of WZBS," he said. "I'm very glad you boys are here!"

"So far we haven't been very much help, I'm afraid," said Winston. "Maybe if we could get the ghosts in one place, we'd have a chance."

"That won't be easy," Mr. Schmidt said. "I just got off the phone with the other station managers in New York. These ghosts are at every other station in the city, too!"

"Hmm," Egon thought aloud. "It would take too long to go from station to station to trap them all. If we could just lure all the ghosts to one studio—say here, perhaps—it would be much easier to trap them. But how?"

"Wait a minute," cried Mr. Schmidt. "I think I have an idea that just might work."

Mr. Schmidt went on the air to make an anouncement. "WZBS is going to present a show called *The Great Ghost Show*," he said. "All ghosts interested in performing are asked to come to the WZBS studios. Thank you."

The Real Ghostbusters planned to trap all the ghosts at once when they arrived at the station.

The announcement worked! Almost immediately, a steady stream of ghosts came from TV stations all over the city. They poured into the great office building that housed the WZBS studios.

The Real Ghostbusters stood ready, hoping their trap would work. Mr. Schmidt kept his fingers crossed, too.

In they came, ghosts of all shapes and sizes, streaming into the studio. There were song-and-dance ghosts with hats and canes, juggling ghosts, acrobat ghosts, magicians pulling ghostly rabbits out of hats. And all these ghosts had just one idea in mind. Each wanted to be the star of WZBS's new program, *The Great Ghost Show*.

Meanwhile, The Real Ghostbusters were ready. They had Ghost Traps set all around the studio. The needle of Egon's PKE Meter went off the scale. "According to my readings, that should be all of them," he said. "They're all here."

"Okay, guys," Peter shouted. "This is it. Ready. Open Ghost Traps and fire Proton Guns. Now!"

Just as The Real Ghostbusters were about to open fire, Mr. Schmidt came running over to them, yelling. "Wait! Wait!" he shouted. "Don't shoot!"

"Why?" asked Peter. "We're all charged up. I mean, we are a well-oiled ghostbusting machine. And you say, 'Wait!' That could be hazardous to our health."

"I have a great idea," explained Mr. Schmidt excitedly. "Since all these ghosts are here anyway, why not let them put on the show for real, broadcast it, and trap them afterward? It can't do any harm, and besides—the ratings will be tremendous!"

The Real Ghostbusters agreed, and the show began. "Live from New York," the announcer proclaimed, "it's *The Great Ghost Show*, the new, all-ghost variety special. And now, let the show begin!"

With that, the ghosts began to show off their various talents. They sang, danced, juggled, did magic tricks, told jokes, and performed every other possible type of entertainment. All in all, the show was a howling success.

Upstairs, in the control room, Mr. Schmidt and The Real Ghostbusters watched the show on a monitor.

"What a hit!" exclaimed Mr. Schmidt. "This is going to be the highest-rated show of the year. I can just feel it."

"The show's almost over," said Winston. "Let's go get ready to trap those ghosts."

"You know, I almost feel sorry for the ghostly little hams," said Ray. "I've always dreamed of being a TV star, myself."

"Don't get sentimental on us now, killer," said Peter. "Come on, let's go. We've got to bust some ghosts!"

The Real Ghostbusters took their positions back in the studio. When the show ended, they prepared to fire their Proton Guns, but they never got the chance. As each ghost took his bow he moved down the line of Real Ghostbusters, shook each of their hands, and then shook Mr. Schmidt's hand.

One by one the ghosts sailed up into the lights and out of the station. Soon the last ghost had gone. WZBS was ghost free, and The Real Ghostbusters hadn't fired a single Proton Stream!

"Idon't get it," said Peter. "They just left. We never even got to show off!"

"I think I understand," said Ray. "Those were the ghosts of folks who had always wanted to be on TV but never had the chance. Lots of people dream of being on TV."

"That makes sense," said Egon. "It explains why they invaded all the TV stations in the first place. Spirits can't rest unless their lifelong dreams are fulfilled. They just wanted to be on TV. You can't really blame them."

Good-byes and thank yous were exchanged, and The Real Ghostbusters headed back to the firehouse.

Back at the firehouse, Peter decided to finish off the Chinese-food leftovers. "I think I've gotten the hang of these things," he said, gripping his chopsticks.

He opened a carton, only to discover that someone had finished all the leftover Chinese food.

"Slimer!" Peter yelled.

And somewhere, hiding in the firehouse, Slimer let out a very loud belch.